Contents

Draw it!
Focus on: aw, **au** as in <u>*saw*</u>, <u>c*au*se</u>..................3

The house mouse
Focus on: ow, **ou** as in <u>*how*</u>, <u>*out*</u>..................12

Look now!
Focus on: ow, **ou** as in <u>*how*</u>, <u>*out*</u>..................17

Phonemes: ch, sh, th, wh, ph, a_e, ai, ay, e_e, ea, ee, y *as e*, i_e, ie, igh, y *as i,* o_e, oa, ow, u_e, ue, oo, ew, ar, or, er, ir, ur, wr, oo, u, oy, oi, <mark>aw, au, ow, ou</mark>
'Tricky' words: my, can't, does, love, here, are, look, our, eyes, house, were, little

About this book

These short stories are designed to give children blending and reading practice. They are decodable, which means the words in them only include letter shapes and sounds that the children have learned. The stories gradually introduce 'tricky' words, building on the learning in the Red Series.

The progression links directly to the teaching order in the Letterland teaching range. Each story begins with a title page that provides important information for children and teachers.

Story title

Focus on: New spelling patterns introduced

New 'tricky' words: Common words with irregular spellings

Basic teaching tips:

- Encourage the sounding out of decodable words (and any decodable parts of 'tricky' words).
- Discuss the stories with the children to ensure comprehension and engagement.
- Encourage re-reading in pairs or individually to develop fluency and reading for meaning.

Red Series introduces the a-z letters and sounds and some 'tricky words'. On completion of this series, the following words remain tricky in part: **a, the, she, oh, for, that, ok, they, says, her, this, to, said, of, what, you, was, want, come, sees, asks, do.** These words are included in **Blue Series**.

Draw it!

Note: Young readers may require help with the word **autumn** which is only partly decodable.

Focus on: aw, au
as in *saw*, *cause*

Dippy Duck loves to draw. She started to draw her duckpond at dawn but she felt something was missing. Clever Cat came over and said, "Maybe it needs some dawn shades."

Clever Cat got some pink and yellow crayons.

She began to fill the sky with the shades of dawn.

Later, Fred saw the drawing. Dippy said, "I think it is still missing something."

Fred added a fawn getting a drink from the pond.

"That's better," said Dippy Duck.

Then, Lucy Lamp Light paused in front of the drawing. "Can I help?" she asked.

"Yes, do!" said Dippy Duck.

"I'll just add a little lizard crawling across the lawn... like that!" she said.

Next the Hat Man hopped up to have a look.

He added a hawk flying over the pond.

More Letterlanders came over.
"We can add autumn leaves to this drawing!"
they said.

Autumn leaves are red and tawny gold.

The Letterlanders gathered in front of Dippy Duck's drawing. "There are lots of good bits in this dawn drawing," Dippy said.

"I can't decide what I like the most.

I think it is AWESOME!"

The house mouse

Focus on: ow, ou
as in *how*, *out*

Hi, my name is Squeaks. I am a house mouse. I live in that round hole. I am proud to have found this house.

But I must keep a look out… sh… What's that noise?

The Mum in this house doesn't like me. She shouted at me and chased me with a brush. The dust got in my mouth!

The dad tried to poison me so I chewed a hole in his trousers!

But the boy – he's okay. He left some cheese for me under the couch. When I grabbed the cheese, he took a photo of me!

I hope he liked my photo. I liked his cheese!

Sh! Oh, that sound is Bow-Wow, the brown hound dog. He growls and tries to chase me, but just bounds around.

Oh no! It's the cat, Miss Frown.

Help! I think she is about to pounce!!

Look now!

Focus on: ow, ou
as in *h<u>ow</u>, <u>ou</u>t*

When the sun shines and there are no clouds, Howard and Jack like to play outside. They run about and ride bikes.

Howard found some round rings for them to sit in on the sea.

Then Mum shouted loudly, "Come in now! It's lunch time."

Howard dropped his ring down onto the ground.

"No, Howard. Pick it up or it might not be around when we get back," said Jack.

Mum had put out a picnic lunch on a towel.
There was fresh trout and a big mound of buns.

The tide was out, but now the tide is in.
"Look now! I can't see the ground! Thanks for telling me to pick up my round ring!" said Howard.

About this series

This series of 10 books accompanies the Letterland teaching range. Each book contains a selection of short stories. In total there are 32 engaging stories featuring the phonic elements listed below as well as some 'tricky' high-frequency words.

Book	Focus elements	As in the word...	Story titles
1	sh, ch, th, th, wh, ph	_ch_ip, _sh_op, _th_at, _th_ing	Check on the chicks Shep and me What is that thing?
2	a_e, ai, ay	m_a_k_e_, r_ai_n, s_ay_,	A safe place Kate bakes a cake Kane's tail!
3	e_e, ea, ee, y	th_e_s_e_, s_ea_, b_ee_, bab_y_	A trip to the sea Mr E's trees Happy!
4	i_e, ie, igh, y	l_i_k_e_, t_ie_, n_igh_t, m_y_	Ben rides his bike Cats at night What a mess!
5	o_e, oa, ow	h_o_m_e_, b_oa_t, sh_ow_	The bad goat When the cold wind blows Lost in the Queen's maze
6	u_e, ue, oo, ew	c_u_b_e_, bl_ue_, m_oo_n, f_ew_, gr_ew_	Stuck on a dune A day at the zoo The Hat Man's new roof
7	ar, or, er, ir, ur, wr	f_ar_m, f_or_, h_er_, g_ir_l, f_ur_, _wr_ite	The big match Snapshots The bird girls My very bad morning
8	o, oo, u, oy, oi	s_o_n, b_oo_k, p_u_t, b_oy_, c_oi_n	Oscar's brother The big pull Nick's noisy new toy
9	aw, au, ow, ou	s_aw_, c_au_se, h_ow_, _ou_t,	Draw it! The house mouse Look now!
10	Review ear, air	p_ear_, y_ear_, f_air_	My shark dream A fresh feast Bears at the fair A fairy story

Collect the sets

Phonics Readers - Red Series

Phonics Readers - Blue Series

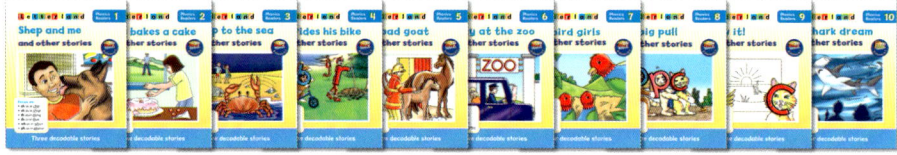

Published by Letterland International Ltd. 8/10 South Street, Epsom, Surrey, KT18 7PF, UK.
www.letterland.com
ISBN: 978-1-78248-188-1
Product Code: TJ10

© Letterland International 2016
LETTERLAND™ is a trademark of Letterland International Ltd.

First published 2013. This new edition published 2016.
Reprinted 2023.
10 9 8 7 6 5 4 3 2

Authors: Stamey Carter and Lisa Holt
Originator of Letterland: Lyn Wendon
Artwork: Baz Rowell
Design: Lisa Holt

The author asserts the moral right to be identified as the author of this work. All rights reserved. No part of this publication may be reproduced, stored in a retrieval system, or transmitted in any form or by any means, electronic, mechanical, photocopying, recording or otherwise, without either the prior permission of the Publisher or a licence permitting restricted copying in the United Kingdom issued by the Copyright Licensing Agency Ltd, 90 Tottenham Court Road, London W1T 4LP. This book is sold subject to the condition that it shall not be by way of trade or otherwise be lent, hired out or otherwise circulated without the Publisher's prior consent.

Printed in Beirut, Lebanon.